An Occasional History

Laura Davenport

Sagging Shorts

Printed in the United States of America.
Set in LTC Garamont with LaTeX.

ISBN: 978-1-944697-38-9 (paperback)
ISBN: 978-1-944697-39-6 (ebook)
Library of Congress Control Number: 2017931958

Sagging Meniscus Press
web: http://www.saggingmeniscus.com/
email: info@saggingmeniscus.com

For Catherine Kasper
who taught me about language

An

Occasional

History

Contents

Examples of
Reconstruction

His voice seems to occupy the length of her arm below the elbow. She cannot bend along predetermined hinges. Ball and socket joints rendered useless. But then there is the folding of knees, legs in a pile; the shape of occupying.

He tells her that the momentum of a swing is kinetic, but she knows nothing of motion. Walking is perpetual; occasionally she attempts to fix movement.

What does it mean to be a unit of sound? This is what she meant to ask that day while leaning against a shopping cart, but instead became distracted by the curvature of broccoli—the echoing of a double consonant within her mouth.

HE ONLY eats crunchy vegetables. Always discards tomatoes, leaves them in a mushy mound on his plate. She drinks through straws, cannot abide liquid against teeth.

She once toyed with the idea of scraping the taste buds from her tongue, even went so far as to map the organ, if only to discover the exact nature of *epithelium*.

He is incapable of understanding the importance of non-vascular tissue. Knows the sensation of legs crossing and uncrossing, of action undone as she enters a room.

THE FOOT presupposes a toe. Legs extend from beneath this space she sometimes occupies. An error is made by walking; he says *hello*. Upon rising, she mumbles something about redundancy but before she can finish he is in the yard balancing a slip of obsidian along his palm. In this movement against gravity she perceives the implication of equatorial boundaries; her body wider at the center, a consequence of rotation.

S HE COLLECTS pieces of chert, traces their chalk-lined edges before placing them in the curve of her bra. (Later he undresses her, lets the rocks fall to the floor, judges their solidity.) When the mosquitoes have settled, they visit the chain-linked fence. He creates points by knapping against the gate, showering her with amorphous silica.

Aɴᴅ ᴀʟᴛʜᴏᴜɢʜ she concerns herself with matters of correspondence, neither to nor from anyone, rather the history of change, one verb into another, she finds she is easily distracted by skin. This largest of organs that he stretches in early afternoon while drifting amongst basalt heads.

WHEN SHE SPEAKS of multiplicities she discovers she lacks the simplest of terms: a flashlight pressed against her ribcage. The complete history of vessels. Her skin rebels, refuses all attempts at transparency.

Theirs is a relationship of light and electrical impulse.

He tells her that all bodies are designed for folding, so he is able to carry her, in sections, and lay her pieces on the couch. Only later, after she has difficulty climbing the stairs to the attic, will they discover that he has somehow forgotten to include a section of her lung—which he keeps in his pocket and squeezes while driving.

SOMEONE HAS SENT her a box, with the word *fragile* stamped across her address. Inside she finds an article on desert mummies whose open mouths stare at her as she reads. She admires the desiccating property of sand; how form remains after burial amongst the grains. Perhaps if he were to find her dead one day he would place her in a bathtub.

Now when she stands she balances on ankles alone. All objects fall at a constant rate, even his name, which she drops off a third floor balcony. Tomorrow someone will trip against the fractured texture of a bilabial stop, but in this moment, pre-descent, the pressure of a name presses.

She likes: lemon curd, couches pushed against walls, winding yarn around her fingers, fossilized impressions, immutable gestures, giant squid.

She fears: freezing water, walking alone, anacamptic tongues, tornadoes and all things conical, coughing on airplanes.

He sleeps with one eye open.

IF SHE were inclined she would lay him across the bathroom floor. He would unfurl his legs, occupying each corner with his extremities; would blush beneath fluorescent lighting. She would wear a smock and thick plastic goggles. And as she slid her hands beneath his shoulder blades, he would whisper: *The Corinthian column is almost always fluted.*

EXACT STATEMENTS trouble her; they leave no room for accidents, no space in which to stumble. Her body is marked by clumsiness: a scar at the knee, scabbed elbows and a bruised spine that aches. They have chosen to paint the walls of their bedroom. This is the form of beige, he says. She remembers the feel of sweaty knees in summer; evenings spent in the front seat of a car, two bodies and a steering wheel.

A sometimes entryway. Two pairs of socks. A living/dining combination. Mismatched plates. Behind wooden cabinets. Water drips into a stainless basin. This door can slide both left and right.

ON A BUS she saw him enter. He chose the seat directly behind the driver and although his hands were not visible, she assumed they were gloved. She wore scarves then, of varying lengths depending on the day. Mondays were equated with a long cable of black wool wound loosely around her neck, obscuring the angle of her chin. The bus was on Thursday, sensible grey cotton. She almost said hello; rose from her seat to walk to the front of the bus. Then she remembered.

WHEN SHE SPEAKS of multiplicities she lacks the simplest of terms.

When she tries to talk about too many things she tends to forget the obvious. When she tries to discuss a variety of subjects she doesn't know how to say what she means. When she tries to compare the linguistic features of different languages she tends to forget the commonplace.

SHE CAN'T REMEMBER the word for *eyelash*; she only remembers what an eye looks like when it is half-closed/half-open/in the process of blinking. She only knows that it is connected to an eye. She can't remember how to say *eyelash* in any language; she understands that it relates to the blinking of an eye/the idea of the blinking of an eye. She is about to say the word *eyelash* but forgets because he is staring at her, distracting her with his blinks/by blinking/with his blinking. She is about to say the word but she doesn't/can't because she is interrupted by the memory/action of an eye frozen/stopped/slowly hanging in the process of blinking.

HER PUPILS contract when he turns on a light, which annoys her. He turns on a lamp, hurts her eyes, causes her pupils to contract. She is bothered by automatic physical responses, such as the contraction of pupils to outside stimuli. She has been trying to learn how to control automatic/unconscious bodily functions/functions governed by the primitive/reptilian brain, but realizes, once he turns on a lamp and her pupils automatically contract, that she cannot.

When/As she bullshits/talks about/discusses/compares/analyzes/tries to/attempts to/speak about/mention too many things/a variety of subjects/two things at once/the linguistic features/words/vocabularies/nuances of different/many/distinct languages she forgets/overlooks/doesn't know how to say/realizes that she has forgotten/can't remember how to say the obvious/what she means/commonplace terms/her own language/every language/words/vocabularies/who she is.

SHE IS in the dark, in the pantry, and he places a flashlight against her ribs. He tries to illuminate the unseen features: her bones, circulatory system, organs, ligaments, etc. Nothing is revealed. (Perhaps because her skin hasn't sufficiently faded.) So instead he imagines he can see the complete workings. She is not in the dark, it is elsewhere where he does this. He imagines he can see every variation that has existed within the confines from pre-embryonic to their present-day states. He imagines he can see everything she has been/is/will be. He imagines she is pregnant (perhaps she is or has been) and he can see her genetic contributions to the developing fetus. He imagines she is pregnant and he can see the transfer of life from her body to the fetus.

T HEIRS is a relationship of light and electrical impulse.

They depend on instances like the turning on of a light and the beating of a heart. They depend on outside stimuli because they don't have anything in common. They don't know how to communicate, so they depend on outside forces in order to interact. They are only concerned with themselves/are consumed by/with/themselves, so they rely on outside/physical impulses to make them aware of/force them to interact with/ each other.

When she speaks of multiplicities she discovers that she lacks the simplest of terms. Once she forgot everything but continued to speak—filling her sentences with odd assortments of sound and not-quite meaning. She pictures the shape of a word before utterance, sometimes to the detriment of its individual components. This is how she speaks:

There was a time when she would allow the shadow of his lashes to distract her. Somewhere a lamp is broken. Here are her eyes, squinting. She imagines the curve, uncurling.

IF SHE WANTED to look at him, she could.

If she wanted to look at him, she would.

If she wanted to explore his body she would touch him.

She would carry him and place his body against the bathroom floor.

She likes to think of herself as strong enough to carry heavy objects.

She holds objects in her mind, never in her hands.

This is what she could do.

This is what she would do.

THEY HAD a mattress on the floor. A bookcase and a lamp. They slept on their sides, spine-pressed. He woke one night to a pool of blood leaking from her body. He wiped her legs with a white cotton washcloth, then carried their bedding to the laundry. Now their bed rests atop a box spring and frame, between head and foot boards. And he sleeps through everything, even running water and the sound of blood sliding across a drain.

SOMETIMES SHE sits like this: On the couch, vertical, never quite touching the cushions. Sometimes she bends, examines her feet, picks at her toenails. He always wears socks, even on the warmest days. They read newspapers, ignoring the pile of dishes in the sink. Sometimes he smiles at her when he enters the room. Sometimes she looks at him and laughs. He brings her coffee. She opens the blinds. They look at the day.

S HE KEEPS her nail file in a drawer, next to a pair of tweezers and a black marker which she uses to make notations on the mirror. Lists of errands, groceries to be purchased, words she finds especially problematic. *Bathtub. Undercurrent. Especially.* He brushes his teeth in the shower, enjoys the sensation of toothpaste spit out across his toes. Often, while shaving, he can't make out the exact shape of his face and erases her writing by smearing it with his palm, and she spends her evenings recreating lists in exact, black letters across the surface of glass.

SHE INSERTS her hands into a pair of rubber gloves and opens the refrigerator. She aligns bottles of condiments in front of the dishwasher. Places a gallon of milk on the floor, thinks that when she is finished she will eat some cheese. He stands next to her, holding a black trash bag. A pint of moldy strawberries, a half-eaten bowl of oatmeal, some expired eggs and a pork loin. These things she drops into the bag. She piles containers of ham and turkey on the counter. He wants her to make a sandwich on toasted rye. But they are out of bread and a jar of pickles has cracked, drenching the cheese in green fluid.

T HE SIDEWALK shadowed in lattice. A shiny beetle moves across concrete. If she were wearing shoes she would crush it with her heel, slide its white interior against the ground. However it is a day of bare feet and sunburned necks, so she nudges the beetle with her toe. Articulated legs wave.

He walks parallel to the column of ants. Across the driveway and into the street. Over two speed bumps to a field. Where he sits next to the body of a sparrow hatchling with sunken eye sockets and exposed wing bones. The ants crawl in and out, small bits of sparrow between their mandibles.

The sky descends onto his arms. He places handfuls of fog in his mouth. With each movement he tastes morning: children crossing the street without looking, the flattened body of a raccoon across a double yellow line. He swallows them all until his belly extends over the lip of his belt. Exhaling slowly, he pushes their undigested remains into the atmosphere.

Teeth consume her thoughts. While walking she feels a twinge in her left bicuspid. She imagines her mouth, toothless. Pictures her voice, lisping. She avoids crunchy vegetables, drinks everything, even water, through a straw. One night she dreams they are in the front yard. He is digging holes in the dirt with a small shovel. While she follows behind, planting broken bits of enamel in neat, parallel rows.

He rearranges objects. Today the bookshelf, which he converts into dry goods storage. On the first shelf: rice and pasta. On the second: canned tomatoes, one tin of tuna. He places a clipboard on the third shelf. This is the food cataloging system, he tells her.

She asks if, perhaps, they could have a pet. He brings her a cactus in a black plastic tub; a card impaled on one of its needles. She sees her name, its second letter pierced through. Fearing small cuts and implied infection, she wears pot holders when watering or removing the shriveled fly carcass that has lain, for nearly a week, within the curve of the cactus.

T HEY STAND at the carts. He pulls one from the cartwell, rolls it forward and back. Pulls out another and another. Lets the discarded carts drift to rest against the entry door. He settles on a small basket with black plastic handles. She tears a list in two, gives him half and walks away, pushing one of the abandoned carts.

The butcher's counter is at the back of the store under a white sign lit with fluorescent lights. MEAT printed in blue block letters. She ignores the arrangement of cuts: rib eye, T-bone, breast, skirt, thigh. Pauses only to press her cheek against the smooth glass case. Stares into the surface of kidneys and tripe before continuing onto the bakery.

The basket is heavy. He wonders if he should return for a cart. But that would require transfer, an unpacking of fruit. He thinks that perhaps the risk of bruising is too great. Decides he should just keep moving, stopping only to collect a bag of flour—the fifth item on his list.

SHE RESCUES spiders. From beneath bathmats. Between blind slats. Behind the dryer. Four daddy longlegs in an inverted drinking glass released onto the balcony. She watches their spindle-quick legs climbing higher into the corner eaves. In the morning she encounters his cologne. Sometimes she imagines his body, bloated and oozing on the bathroom floor.

He washes dishes in the sink. Says he cannot trust the dishwasher. Pots must be left to soak overnight. And then there is the matter of rinsing: glasses first, then plates. She stares into the cabinets, remembering the first dish ever broken.

She considers what it means to be a body pressed into carpet. He stretches up and down, balances on the balls of his feet. She thinks he is learning to creep, to uncreate noise. One morning she will wake to the shape of his face, looming.

An Interlude
Among Strangers

Or

She Sits on the Bathroom Floor

Reading Romance Novels

Why all this need for hiding?

Clayton has purchased her from her father. Or, rather, her father (who is heavily in debt) has, unbeknownst to his own daughter, affianced her to Clayton. The terms: an erasure of debt in exchange for a bride.

Who is our hero?

A duke in disguise. Because Whitney should fall in love with a common man, she should not be swayed by his title or be wary of his reputation with women. And she should never know the terms of their betrothal contract.

How do events complicate?

Whitney loves another. Or at least she believes she always has.

Her father has loose lips.

She does, in all actuality, love the duke in disguise.

And what of the body?

Summer's hair shines long and black. But when she is released from Newgate it is cropped short, a series of curls against her ears. Her husband, Ruark, longs to touch her, but her skin is transparent; her bones breakable.

How, then, can he be both Gentleman and Pirate?

Unbeknownst to his wife, Ruark and Rory are not brothers. An eye patch and a bit of boot blacking applied to the hair can transform one individual into two. So, in the most basic way, Summer has never been unfaithful.

What do they want?

To master. To ravish. To seduce. To manipulate. To love. To satiate. To lie naked in a hammock.

Sometimes things are different; how?

Perhaps Judith is a bit wicked. She is a widow after all. But her solitude is not one of chastity. The matter of virginity has long been discarded. And she collects orchids, has constructed a hothouse in London.

But what is always the same?

A touch that burns. Two sideways glances. Gideon's body falling into hers.

How did it all begin?

Perhaps it was the flash of blue skirt or the need for fresh air. Or maybe the intersection of two gloved hands.

What do his fingertips find?

The slope of her shoulder, a length of arm extended. This Marcus is shocking, dares to trace her spine with his tongue.

How does he come to her rescue?

Once, he saves her from a baked calf's head; from slices of steaming tongue. Lillian thinks, later, he will kiss her.

And later?

She sinks into the curve of his hip bones against her lower back, her body cradled within his.

What is the Secret Passion of Simon Blackwell?

Parchments and vellum. Illuminated manuscripts. And one Lady Annabel McBride.

How does he fill his nights?

Whiskey. Endless journal entries. Sometimes falling asleep in chairs.

Later.

With her.

And what does she discover?

That a man can't kiss like that and feel nothing.

Where is the unique?

Claire's first taste of yogurt. Trevelyan's first battle with jealousy. The first time she whispers his name, feels their bodies arching.

What has Vellie done?

Returned from the dead.

Stolen his brother's fiancée.

Worn the laird's plaid.

What is in the trunks?

Letters. Hundreds of them. In bundles tied with ribbon. Secret words of the true duke. The one Claire loves.

What is discarded?

Her spinster ways. Alone at not-quite-thirty, Xanthia Neville decides to embark on an affair.

Whom does she tempt?

Stefan, the Marquess of Nash, a perhaps spy and rake extraordinaire.

How does he declare?

By scaling her garden wall and speaking of a line now drawn: marriage or nothing.

Where is the dilemma?

To wed for duty? Or, to wed for love? Only the seventh Earl of Sachse can decide.

On whom can he depend?

Countess Camilla, his predecessor's widow. Her beauty is thorough, her countenance remote.

What is revealed?

The Countess cannot read. The Earl is not the earl. And they can spend hours together beneath a tree, the weight of their bodies cresting.

What is craved?

The most proper woman always desires an uncivilized man. Emeline Gordon, widow and chaperone, seduced by a sensuous mouth.

How does he escape?

Samuel runs for hours: through the woods beyond the manor's boundaries, across cobblestones into the London night.

Where is soothing?

Her fingers against his bloodied feet. The whisper of lemon balm on her flesh.

How does it begin?

On a moonlit night with a masked stranger. A breathless kiss exchanged.

How does it really begin?

Ten years earlier, Nicola spurns the Earl of Exmoor in favor of one of his grooms. And the stable hand, one Gil Martin, will pay with his life.

Now that Gil has returned from the dead, what will Nicola risk?

Everything.

An Occasional History

The Pelvic Bone
and its Residual Tail

S HE DOESN'T recognize this latest bruise, a purple
half-moon on her upper thigh. Then there is the
splatter burn on her chest—two drops of hot mint
tea against her collarbone. Perhaps she should be concerned. Instead, she thinks *this body is not mine.*

When she was younger, she reached into the honeysuckle vines on her grandmother's front porch trellis.
She can't recall now if that was the year of the rabid
cattle dog. The series of endless shots—the beginning
of preoccupation with blood-borne illnesses.

Once, as she bent to pick a flower from the vine, she
leaned in too close and brushed against the plant with
her eye. When she straightened her body, she realized a piece of the plant was lodged in the white of
her eyeball. She imagined a series of vines springing
forth from her face, cascading down her body, tak-
ing root in the ground. She would disappear into the
plant and although her mother might notice the new
vine in the backyard and might realize her daughter
had gone missing, she would never associate the two
events as one singular experience. Quickly, the girl
pulled the twig from her eye. Now, this many years

later, a brown spot persists between the curve of her iris and the fleshy pink membrane of her lacrimal caruncle.

The cat sat hiding, flicking his tail into the leaves of the honeysuckle. She harbored a secret disdain for cats, could not explain now, if so compelled, what exactly obligated her to extend her arm outwards, into the trellis. Perhaps she had not heard the humming, or had discounted it as nothing more than the buzzing of chicharas at dusk or the crackling of the bug zapper.

WHEN THEIR mattress was on the floor, he would climb over her body, leave for work. She would roll closer to the wall. In her dreams a man would pick the lock on the front door and would find her sleeping body. He would stand over her as he disrobed before lowering himself on the bed to pull her legs apart with calloused palms and bury himself deeper and deeper. Later she would search for answers; sometimes she would spend hours standing next to a chair on the covered patio, trying to imagine the shape of subconscious rape. She began to question whether her mind was failing her. So she began waking earlier, sitting with her back against the wall, naked with legs spread in open invitation: a means to avoid rape.

SHE FELT the flutter of wings first. Against her upper right forearm. And then the sear of stingers. The sensation of countless bodies piercing her own. With her left hand, she lifted a portion of the vine and leaned in closer to watch. She saw her arm begin to swell and observed the creation of welts rising.

SHE THINKS *rape* is a woman's word. *Miscarriage.* *Virginity.* She mouths these words, forms the shape of their sounds with her lips. And then there are pain words. *Bag. Water.*

H ER GREAT AUNT was the one who found her, dizzy on the front porch. Arm leadened by the weight of yellow jackets. She leaned into the house, stared as her aunt bit her still-lit cigarette in two, and slowly chewed. Then spit bits of brown tobacco onto her arm. *There*, her aunt said, *you'll be right as rain tomorrow.*

Today she is standing in her friend's kitchen, watching him pull gizzards from the body cavity of a raw chicken. A bit of watery blood splashes onto her thumb; she resists the urge to lick it off. He asks her if she knows how to judge whether the chicken is done cooking. *By turning the thigh like so.*

There are two grackles fighting over a piece of bread. She wants to throw her chair at them. They stare at her, heads turning slowly from side to side, daring her. Instead, she sits, unmoving, and thinks that the only bird more terrifying than a grackle is a crow. Thankfully no crows live here.

As she walks to her car she hears a mourning dove. Or maybe a mockingbird.

T HE FIRST TIME she dreamt of the funnel cloud it was black and racing down the street. She tasted dust, ran in a zigzag pattern into a dry creek bed, where she pressed her body into the earth and felt the tip of the tornado tickle her spine.

She used to fall asleep on the couch and wait for the phone to ring. Then she would drive across town, worrying about the state of her legs or the book she should be reading. But never about the solitary walk from his front door, down four flights of stairs, back to her car.

Sometimes she would float in the eye of the funnel, would watch planks of wood flash past. Bits of roof or tree roots. Other times, the pressure of the wind would separate her body at the joints. She would see her hand slip from her wrist.

Sometimes they would shower. Sometimes she would just watch. Always they would end up on his living room floor, where she once forgot about the gum in her mouth and found it in a tangle at the base of her skull. Which he cut out with orange-handled scissors while she moved her head up and down, tracing the length of his penis with her tongue.

Often, the tornado would just cease and she would fall from the sky only to crash down into broken window panes or bent fence posts. She would dust the aftermath of storm from her skin. Walking, with lilting steps, back from whence she came.

Or sometimes on his bed, which smelled of dryer sheets, where he would reach between her legs with his fingers and, occasionally, his mouth. Always she would decline, having not yet learned to be unafraid of pleasure. And once on his kitchen counter where she broke a spice rack with a careless thrust of her arm.

If the tornado arrived on a hot August night, the winds would singe. She would smolder before erupting into flames. An occasional charred bone would float to the grass below.

And then one night in someone else's bathroom. Afterwards, he zipped his pants and left her alone so that his friend, who had been waiting (ear pressed against the door) could enter; grab her head, push it into his body.

IN FIRST GRADE, her teacher asked the class to draw a picture of a thesaurus. While everyone else drew long-limbed, wide-jawed dinosaurs, she drew a picture of a book, which infuriated her teacher.

SHE SAW a man trip in the rain and poke the woman in front of him with the point of his umbrella. Once she read about a man who was felled by the toxicity of the castor bean. Assassinated when the tip of an umbrella, dipped in castor bean oil, pierced his skin.

He helped her with complex verb forms. In the morning while they stood, arms touching, at the balcony railing. He would sip from her tea and create long phrases that she would repeat. She kept the conjugations of past subjunctives and pluperfects inside her mouth.

When she was twelve, she rummaged through her grandmother's sewing box in search of a thimble. Her fingers stumbled across the curve of a bean. Its surface warm and oily. She slid the bean along her palm then wrote her name on her thigh, using its unctuous quality as ink.

He gave her a key. She ordered soup for them in roadside diners and they went on long walks before breakfast. After a year she realized that the verbs exchanged were always his. The shape of her language became tangled in his mouth so that even the simplest of sentences escaped him.

That night she could feel the oil seeping into her pores; her thigh began to burn. She re-remembered the secret poison of the castor bean. And as such, spent the next few days anticipating an agonizing death that was never to come.

H ER TOWN LIBRARY was small and too far from home to be reached by bike. So her mother would drive. One summer she only read books about alien abductions. She would walk into the pasture behind the house, where she would read and watch scissor-tails cut across the sky.

She met a man from London who played the fiddle. He had a crooked smile and smooth, ivory skin. She told him that he played honky-tonk with a British accent. He tapped her on the shoulder with his bow, suggested they take a walk. Then smiled at her, sideways.

When she checked out books, she would always be sure to have a variety of other subjects in which to hide: native trees, home remedies, aviation advances of the past fifty years, the War of 1812. She would intersperse her tales of people stolen from their homes at night by creatures with large eyes and pale orbed skin. She was afraid that someone would notice her preoccupation with other-worldly abductions. That the librarian might, perhaps, inquire.

That first night they exchanged names, then palms. He held her hand across twelve city blocks. She smiled; he commented on the whiteness of her teeth. Finally, they sat on a bench.

Her mother selected the arrangement of her room and so her bed was situated between two windows. She would have preferred it to be across the room, against the opposite wall. So if aliens were to come she would see their arrival and have time to prepare.

THEY FELL ASLEEP holding hands. In the morning, he walked her to her car, kissed the corner of her mouth. The imprint of his lips could still be felt that night as they sat across from each other, eating barbeque with their fingers.

The aliens never arrived. She began to worry that something was amiss, that she was not perfect enough. When fall announced itself by the turning of grass from green to brown, she stopped visiting the library.

She lay next to him, imagined her body as a fiddle.

By winter she was reading again. But only books about Victorian orphans, or girls with long hair and backyard swings.

When it came time for him to leave, to fly back home, he invited her to sit next to him. *My fear of airplanes is too great* she said.

The next summer, she read over one hundred books. The librarian hung her picture on the wall, behind the circulation desk.

Had she been honest, she would have said that the curl of her name on his voice brought her comfort like no other.

By spring she had read all the authors from A-M.

ONE DAY she found herself across the ocean. She called him from a payphone next to a tobacco shop. She felt the tickle of his voice against the receiver before she hung up, having heard a woman speak his name as if from over his shoulder.

She had always been tiny. Then one day she was not.

SHE WAS CONVINCED she would accidentally set herself afire while pumping gas. Or perhaps fall asleep in the bathtub and drown. She could have choked while eating alone in her house.

A man called out another's name when she was atop him. One convinced her to leave her underwear in a fountain downtown after having pressed his fingers so high into her that she spotted blood for five days. And then there was the man who would let her sleep next to him. Who would pull her hair away from her face and whisper nursery rhymes against her ear until she fell asleep.

SHE DOES NOT have red hair that falls in fat ringlets down her back. Or dark eyes that snap you in daylight. She does not laugh easily and cannot reach the top shelf even when standing on tiptoes. Her ankles are not dainty; neither her wrists. Her saving grace: small, white teeth, perfect in their alignment.

AFTER SHE gave birth, she didn't want to hold her baby. The nurses kept asking. She always said no, afraid that he would look at her and she would see censure in his unfocused eyes. Even now, she worries that one day he will remember everything he observed through the wall of her stomach. When he comes into her room at night and asks for a glass of water, she cannot help but worry that someday he will know. And he will never ask her for anything again.

A WOMAN at the table next to her says, *People do not want to hear about your experiences. Not in that voice.* She wants to scream, to say she has not spoken in days. Instead, she drinks tea through an overly-long straw, before unfolding her legs to stand and walk across the room.

IF SHE allows herself, she can picture the night she ceased to be human. Hands against her windpipe, his voice in her ear. Sticky breath words. But he didn't kill her then. Or later. Not even when he pinned her on the couch or threw blunt objects at her head. She thinks maybe he didn't hate her sufficiently to try hard enough. She thinks that, like a cockroach, she has been living for years without her head. One day she will die of thirst.

S HE IS GOING to be late. Perhaps she is already. Her
friends are waiting, sitting outside in the car.
Through the open window, she can hear the echo
of footsteps on the sidewalk against the first leaves
of fall. She shrugs into her jacket, slides her arms
into the sleeves. Thinks she should be hurrying. He
is leaning against the kitchen counter, picking at
a hole in the formica with his thumbnail. Beyond
him, the front door. *You should be more careful with hot
pans*, he says. This is the second time she's burned the
counter. She knows she should answer. Then kiss his
cheek and slip past. But she is hurrying, doesn't pause
to consider her words. Says, *I'm late*. Maybe the tone
was incorrect. Or her jacket's hem scraped against
his leg too roughly. He grabs her wrist, squeezes until her hand becomes purple. She should just stand
still, let the pressure subside, but she is late; so she
attempts to twist her wrist from between his hand.
Everything's a fight with you, he says before releasing
her. She walks past, turns the deadbolt. Listens for
the tumble of the lock unlocking. He is listening too,
grabs her jacket collar, pulls her downward. She hears
the seams popping and thinks maybe she can extri-

cate herself from this khaki pea coat and rush out the door; but her shoulders are too broad. He pushes her across the kitchen floor. She feels her jeans rip at the knee. She tells him her friends are waiting outside. He tells her that no one will hear. His fingers at her waistband, tugging. The zipper descends. His pants have disappeared into a pile at his ankles. She tries to crawl away; tries to rezip; tries to yell out the window, across the parking lot and into her friends' car. But his hands are many, pushing against her mouth. She feels the slicing of flesh, imagines the layers of vaginal skin beneath jagged nails. Wonders if later, while washing his hands, he will scrub his fingers with a nailbrush. She thinks one day she will need stitches, will be forced to invent a story while sitting, both feet in stirrups, as a gynecologist sews her back together. He spits into his palm, rubs his penis before thrusting into her, elbows on either side of her head. When he finishes, he collapses atop, kisses her eyelids, whispers that she better hurry. She shouldn't be late.

The beauty of this apartment, he tells her one day while she is organizing photos on the hallway floor, *is that we are practically underground.* She is placing the photos in neat piles, separated according to chronology, tells him *Yes, we save a lot of money on our heating bill.* He nods and walks into the bedroom. Her fingers tremble; she wills them to stop by focusing on a picture of her former self. She wraps each photo-pile with a rubber band, places them in a box on the top shelf of the linen closet. And as she grabs a towel from the second shelf, she acknowledges that the true beauty of an apartment such as this is the way that sound is absorbed, that even the loudest of screams is muffled by the layers of earth, surrounding.

SHE HAS HAD the same two feather pillows since she was three. Sometimes, when her right cheek is pressed into the topmost pillow, she tries to peer beneath the surface, into the mass of feathers and imagine the consequence of sleeping atop more than two decades of sloughed skin. At times she can hear the whisper of mites, crunching. He is snoring. She closes her eyes, focuses on the shape of the underside of her eyelids. Two hours pass. He snores still. She nudges him. Grabs his thigh with her hand. Sits up, leans over him. Pinches his nostrils shut. He snores on. She rolls over. Makes a list of irregular verbs, whispers them into her pillow. *Arise. Backslide. Creep. Mislay.* She rolls over again. Then turns onto her back. This movement startles. He hovers above; she closes her eyes. Feels the breeze of his palm before the slap. All morning he says the word *sorry*. And she is forced to wear sunglasses at work for the next week.

Things he has said while sitting next to her with a knife: I'll kill you first, then myself; You force me to do this, you know; Sometimes you make me so mad.

Things he has said while pressing, gently, against her windpipe: I know what I'm doing; There is no point in yelling; Sometimes you make me so mad.

Things he has said while hitting: Kidneys damage easily; I'd hold still if I were you; Sometimes you make me so mad.

S HE DOESN'T understand why the slightest bump of her knee against a file cabinet or the intersection of a careless elbow and a doorframe as she turns the corner always leave the most substantial of marks. While a punch to the lower back or a book thrown against her head passes with little notice. Maybe she has been sleeping for this many years. Maybe he has never touched her skin with hands or objects. Perhaps he is to be believed, after all.

She feels her body stretching and thinks her skin will explode. Thirty-six weeks of waiting, clutching her stomach between her hands. Baths provide the only respite from this sensation of overbearing cumbersomeness. She can almost float and pretend she is weightless. He wants to take a shower, but she is lounging. She'd like to tell him that this space is hers, but starts to rise instead. Her movements are sloppy; her balance, compromised. She slips, splashes water onto his leather shoes. He stares at his feet, then throws a shampoo bottle at her stomach. It bounces off her skin. The fetus turns. Her lower back contracts. She tries to stand again. He grabs his beer from the counter, next to the sink. It grazes her right temple before exploding, showering the ceiling with yellowish foam, which drips down the walls, sliding into her eyes.

H ER MOTHER almost died birthing her. She turned purple then blue. The doctor stared at her infant-self as he scraped mucous from her mouth, made a *tisk-tisking* sound. Her mother started breathing again and the *tisk-tisking* took up residence in a secret curve of her eardrum.

What she first noticed were his eyelashes and the fact that he wore long-sleeved plaid shirts, even in summer. Shirts with snaps instead of buttons and always the same pair of ratty loafers. He leaned across the aisle one day in class while everyone else was discussing *The Death of Virgil* and she was mouthing the word *ping*, attempting to stretch out the *ing*, to let it vibrate against the roof of her mouth. *I'd really like to fuck you*, he said.

And what if her mother had died? She considers this often, wonders what it would be like to be a woman marked by public Tragedy. She thinks she would have reveled in it. Would have enjoyed the furtive whispers as she walked down the street or when she ordered a malt at Rexall. *Poor child, tisk-tisk; she killed her mother, you know.*

She told him she was busy that night, maybe tomorrow. Somewhere, she acknowledged that naught could be gained from a man who wore slip-on shoes and could not be bothered with buttons. Instead, they began fucking and she pretended not to notice the way he slammed the refrigerator door or how he sat on the corner of her mattress, drinking gin directly from the bottle.

She thinks that before you feel sorry for her, you should remember that her mother did not die.

H E IS SITTING in the only chair in the living room. She is on the couch, reading. Their son is asleep in the next room. She can hear him coughing. She looks across the space between them. He is watching tv. Feels her momentary glance in his direction. She turns back to her book. He makes it across the room before she can let the novel fall from her lap. Somehow he has a toy truck in his hand. He is beating her cheek with the plastic wheels. Is beating her cheek. Is beating her cheek. Is beating her cheek. Is beating her cheek.

That night she leaves. As she buckles her son into his car seat, she whispers.

I'm sorry. I'm so sorry. I'm so, so sorry.

(Having heard this herself. Many times before.)

Years ago, while reading a newspaper at work, she stumbled across the history of a troupe of baboons in Saudi Arabia. An unidentified car, which she likes to imagine as a late-model four-door sedan, hit one of the baboons and left her for dead. The remaining members of the clan returned to the scene of the murder daily. Until finally, the car came rushing down the road again. And the baboons began pelting the vehicle with rocks and clumps of dirt, while others stormed the car, jumped onto the hood to pound at the windshield with their fists. She hopes if he were to ever kill her that you would do the same.

Memories
of the Future

S HE HAS BEEN concerned with the accidental. The way in which a favorite lost glove rematerializes beneath a chair when she bends to pick a book up off the floor or the time she slipped down a flight of stairs only to land on her feet. But when she waits alone at a bus stop or while standing in line at the grocery store, she allows herself to consider the purposeful.

He sometimes walks. From the living room down the hallway to the linen closet, turn, down the hallway to the living room, turn. She counts his steps and concentrates on invisibility.

They walk from the living room down the hallway to the linen closet. Turn and enter the bedroom. She knows to remove her clothes. Shirt, then bra. To lift her skirt and slide her underwear down her legs. He stands, watching, and when they are naked he places her fingers around his penis. These actions are performed in silence. He presses into her intercostal spaces with his fingers, squeezing and then pushes her onto the bed. Her head grazes the wall before coming to rest against the pillows. He traces her collarbone with his tongue, then pulls her legs apart. She smells his breath, shifts her face to the side. He pinches her nostrils shut and covers her mouth with his palm. When she is dizzy, he lifts his hands so she can gasp. Then exhale. She feels his teeth on her breasts, the slide of saliva. He forces himself inside her. She experiences the tear of skin. He comments on her dryness as he presses in. Her bladder bruises. There will be blood. With his forearm against her windpipe he whispers about the morning she may not live to inhabit. She watches his hips lift and descend, fixated on their bodies joining. Beneath him she thinks *Some good must come of this.* He stays within her until he is flaccid and then rolls over. She wants to kill him, wants to press a pillow against his face while he is snoring or take a knife from the butcher block on the kitchen counter and slice gashes into his chest. Instead, she stays there, on her back, and pulls her knees into her chest, pressing her legs together. She pictures a baby, smaller than a pea, floating in the middle of her belly. Weeks later she wakes up, vomiting.

Certain Words
Are Universal

Rape

rep- to snatch.

Suffixed zero-grade form **rap-yo*. In Latin, *rapere*, to seize:

An object or person seized/ taken by force:

A woman pulled down/ torn/ plundered/ despoiled:

Enraptured/ transported:

With delight.

She imagines a woman on a windswept steppe. Perhaps she has ventured out in search of medicinal herbs or maybe she felt the need to stretch her legs. She walks through knee-high stalks to a stream where she bends to scoop water into her palm. As she swallows she realizes she is not alone so she turns her head, sees a man stalking forth. She starts to run, but his legs are longer. He snatches her from behind. And as such this root has endured centuries with little change.

In front of the mirror she examines her ten-year old body. As she pulls her nightgown over her head, she thinks someday a man will put himself inside of her and then later a baby will slide out. That night she dreams she is in her parents' car. She is sitting behind her mother, who rests her arm against the rolled-down window of the passenger side. Her father presses on the brake. They roll to a stop. She wishes her window were down too, feels the heat of the seat seeping into her thighs. Out of the corner of her eye she sees a man walking toward the car. He reaches into the front seat and pulls her mother out. She grabs for her mother while yelling at her father, who notices nothing, save the red light. When it changes to green, he drives on. She stares out the back windshield and sees her mother being dragged around the corner by her arms. The next morning she brushes her teeth and thinks that is what is meant by rape.

A friend pulled into an alley while standing in line outside a bar. Another while waiting for the bus. One while walking to the library. Or pushing a grocery cart to her car. While hiking in Peru. On the way to school. At a party. On a date. In the shower at the gym. In her bedroom, a window carelessly left open.

She used to fear sleep, was afraid she would wake to the pressure of his body against hers. He would press on endlessly. In the mornings she would use her fingers to scrape away all evidence from the inside. Now she fears strange men on elevators and always remembers to look beneath her car and through the backseat window before unlocking the door.

HYMEN

syū- to bind, sew. Suffixed shortened form
*syu-men, in Greek *humēn*, thin skin,
membrane

Virginal skin stretched across an enclo-
sure.

Also, the Greek god of marriage.

From this: SEW, SEAM, SUTURE,
COUTURE, SUBULATE, SUTRA,
KAMASUTRA, HYMEN

At recess she would sit with friends and they would
braid each others' hair. One day her grandmother
took her to the beauty parlor. The scissors slipped,
eight inches cut. The next day, her friends laughed.
One pointed to the group of boys playing tetherball,

said *Why don't you go over there*, while flicking the tail of her braid.

She likes to imagine she is still a virgin. That her skin has not stretched to accommodate a man's. She wonders what you will think now that you know this. Will you laugh or secretly agree?

Hers will break one day when she falls off her bike and lands on the frame. Years later she and her friends will lose theirs at a party. Everyone, save her, will speak of blood. When she tells them of the absence of red spots against the sleeping bag, she will know her body has failed.

She finds no comfort in nudity. Her nipples are not small and pink. She dreads the removal of her bra, knows her breasts will collapse against her ribcage. She thinks the next man to see her naked will become fixated on the curve of her stomach and will rise from the bed without speaking.

MENSTRUATE

mē (2)—to measure. Contracted from
*mæ. Latin *mēnsis*, month.

Blood flow manifesting in measurable
intervals. Usually of 28 days.

Stains on underwear, jogging shorts, skirts,
the back of a dress, seat cushions, etc.

Some women bleed with the moon. Not her. Having
no fixed cycle of shedding, she desires another word.
One that holds no association with this ancient and
universal unit of time. Sometimes she wishes she had
been born a man.

She would be embarrassed for you to know that she
used to bleed for eight days. Semi-monthly for more

than ten years. Her pelvic muscles would spasm. Then contract. She had to line her bed with beach towels.

One day the bleeding ceased. This absence persisted for years. She would check the calendar hanging on the fridge, waiting for reappearance. It was then that she began to wonder if she could no longer be considered a woman and if others could tell just by looking.

She recalls what she was never told. The pressure of squeezing a body from her own would be easily forgotten, she expected, and the pain of organs settling. But that all she could do was sit and cry. This is what she wishes you had prepared her for.

CARESS

kā- to like, desire. Latin *cārus*, dear.

To treat.

To pet.

To touch.

To stroke.

To fondle.

To blandish.

Affectionately.

She traces her fingers along the plexiglas display cases in the main room before entering the chamber which had housed the women and children during the echoey nights of siege. She feels the space of many hands against her legs, grasping at her skirt.

She goes to dinner with two friends. They are in love. She drinks sparkling water through a straw. The three of them sit at a round table, knees almost touching. Her friend laughs and leans her head into his shoulder. While he traces her fingers with his own. They kiss. She wants to tell them to stop, but knows that these gestures have meaning.

Her son does not like to be held. He wants no hugs and shrugs off kisses. He will only hold her hand to cross the street and will not crawl into her lap when she reads him a story. He would rather sit on the floor. She blames herself.

CONQUER

[*quaerere*]—to seek. Earliest form *quais*.
Latin verb of unknown origin.

By effort or force.

By subjugation.

By fighting.

By struggle.

By opposition.

By mastery.

When the doctor tells her she is pregnant, she is eating a sandwich. She orders a glass of wine then calls him. He says, *Thank you for ruining my day.*

The next morning he apologizes by giving her a card. On its cover, the image of a bear holding a pink heart. Inside, *Have a Beary Happy Valentine!* It is a Thursday in July.

She knows if he were to read this he would tell you she has been mistaken. He would want you to know that she cannot be trusted.

UTERUS

udero- abdomen, womb, stomach. With distinctly similar forms (perhaps taboo deformations) in various languages.

In primates, the organ of gestation, of conception, development, and protection.

What she enjoyed: resting books atop her stomach; eating strawberries; wearing baggy pants; hearing his heartbeat; the first flickers of movement.

What she disliked: everything else.

During her pregnancy she had a calendar which charted fetal development. *Today my arms are as long as this letter i. My eyelashes have sprouted! I have a bladder now. I can hear your voice when you speak.*

Having sheltered another between her cervix and abdominal walls, has she now served her purpose? If her skin had never known the sensation of small feet against her diaphragm, would you consider her incomplete?

She thinks the outline of a foot or wrist might be visible if only enough light were applied.

WHORE

kā- to like, desire. Germanic **hōraz* (feminine **hōrōn*) one who desires, adulterer. Old English *hōre*, whore.

One who desires (female).

To be free of language. To have no need of words. To sit in a room without speaking.

To a man whose skin seeped whiskey. To a man whose hands knew only fists. To a man whose fingers spanned the width of her neck. For five years she forgot how to speak. Forgot how to keep her legs shut. For five years she could not breathe.

He used to smell her underwear when she came home. Even if she had just returned from a trip to the mailbox at the end of the hallway.

No matter how often she bathes, she always senses his imprint between her thighs.

$\left\{\begin{array}{l} \textbf{SHE} \\[1em] \textit{so-} \text{ this, that (nominative). Feminine form} \\ \textit{*syā} \text{ in Germanic *sjō in Old English sēo,} \\ \textit{sīe, she.} \\[1em] \text{Female, woman, lady, lady-love. An im-} \\ \text{material thing whose formation requires} \\ \text{the he for completion.} \end{array}\right\}$

She is something implied or easily identified. When speaking of her, you could easily say *this* or *that*: This is marked by bruises. That walks across the room.

She has no name. She once responded to a series of consonants and vowels. Would say *present* when they were pronounced. Now she recognizes herself in *she*:

She makes me do this. She is unbearable. When alone with him, *you* will also suffice, as in: You make me do this.

One day she will tell her name.

HYSTERIA

udero- abdomen, womb, stomach. Latin *uterus*, womb. Variant form **ud-tero-* in Greek *hustera*, womb, hysteric.

Any weakness of the mind lies at the opening of the womb. To be a woman is to be marked by hysteria.

She laughs aloud as she reads this. As should you.

She imagines speaking. Wonders what would happen if someone were to stop her in a stairwell and ask how she has been, but she knows her mouth knows only the shape of *Fine*.

He says no one would trust her if she were to tell.

She believes him when he says this.

The wind blows napkins across the table. She laughs while picking them up from off the sidewalk. Her friend is drinking coffee; she stirs her tea with a small spoon. They wear sunglasses and talk about newly-formed lines at the corners of their eyes, of the way shoes pinch, their sisters, and the old woman with a grey dog waiting to cross the street. They watch people enter and leave. Eat blueberry muffins. Get up to go to the bathroom. They sit in chairs with no arms. While drinking her tea, she speaks of terror. Her friend hands her a napkin, says *I know*.

Textual Acknowledgements

In the section titled *An Interlude Among Strangers*, the following list of romance novels referenced corresponds to the questions in bold in the following order:

McNaught, Judith. *Whitney, My Love*. New York: Pocket, 2006.
Henley, Virginia. *The Pirate and the Pagan*. New York: Dell, 1990.
Alexander, Victoria. *A Little Bit Wicked*. New York: Avon, 2006.
Kleypas, Lisa. *It Happened One Autumn*. New York: Avon, 2006.
James, Samantha. *The Secret Passion of Simon Blackwell*. New York: Avon, 2007.
Deveraux, Jude. *The Duchess*. New York: Pocket, 1992.
Carlyle, Liz. *Never Lie to a Lady*. New York: Pocket, 2007.
Heath, Lorraine. *As an Earl Desires*. New York: Avon, 2007.
Hoyt, Elizabeth. *To Taste Temptation*. New York: Forever, 2008.
Camp, Candace. *No Other Love*. New York: Harlequin, 2007.

In the section titled *Certain Words are Universal*, etymologies are derived from *The American Heritage Dictionary of Indo-European Roots*, and definitions from *The Oxford English Dictionary*.

Excerpts from *An Interlude Among Strangers* were published in Trickhouse vol. 6.

Special thanks to Laird Hunt whose guidance and unwavering support I will never be able to repay. To Selah Saterstrom, without whom this text, and so much more, would not exist. And a very grateful thank you to Sara Veglahn for her friendship and assistance across countless drafts, cups of chai, and, eventually, state lines.

Laura Davenport holds a PhD in Literature and Writing from The University of Denver. She lives, writes and teaches in San Antonio, Texas.